TOP THAT

Licensed exclusively to Top That Publishing Ltd
Tide Mill Way, Woodbridge, Suffolk, IP12 1AP, UK
www.topthatpublishing.com
Copyright © 2015 Tide Mill Media
All rights reserved
0 2 4 6 8 9 7 5 3 1
Manufactured in China

Written by Joshua George
Illustrated by Puy Pinillos

ISBN 978-1-78445-287-2

A catalogue record for this book is available from the British Library

For Nuala, the littlest fish in the family.

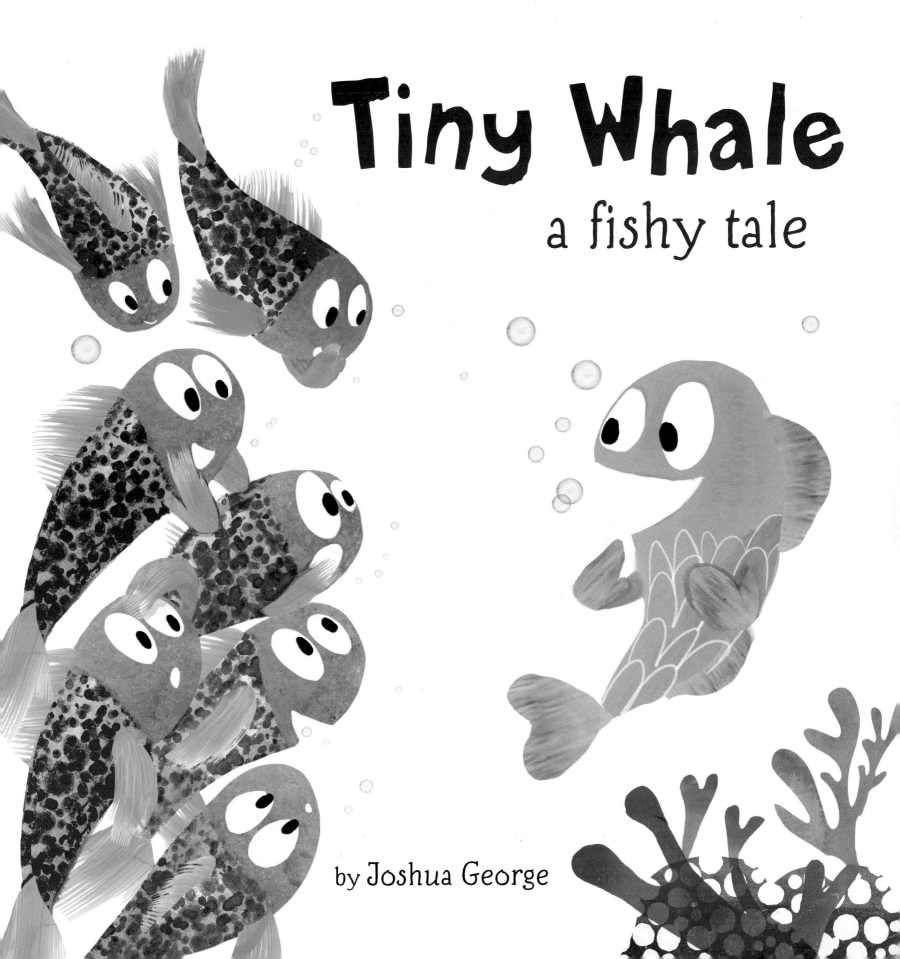

Tiny Whale

a fishy tale

by Joshua George

Gerald had so many brothers, sisters and cousins, that he felt quite unimportant. His dad hardly ever took him to play in the seaweed forest. His mum hardly ever read him stories. Even his best friend Gordon didn't remember his name.

'Hi Gordon!'

'Hi Gavin!'

Gerald   Gavin

'Unbelievable,' thought Gerald.
'I look completely different to Gavin.'

Gerald was tired of being a small orange fish on a reef full of other small orange fish.

So, one day, Gerald decided
to set off on an adventure.

'Goodbye Mum.'

'Goodbye, Gareth.'

'Ridiculous,' thought Gerald.
I look completely different to Gareth.'

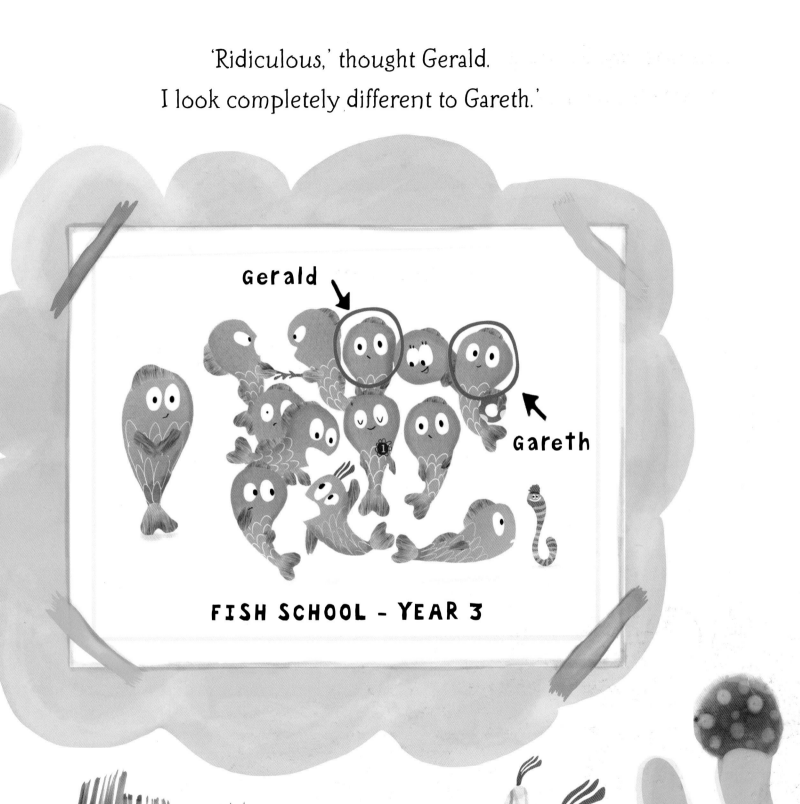

Gerald

Gareth

FISH SCHOOL – YEAR 3

After a long, tiring and scary swim ...

... Gerald finally found himself at another reef.
He was glad to be somewhere safe.

The reef looked like the one at home,
but the fish were blue, not orange.
As Gerald rested, he watched a group
of fish playing hide-and-seek.

'**Hey,**' one of the blue fish shouted.
'I'm Charlie. These are my friends,
Chuck, Chip, Chad and Chet.
What sort of fish are you?'

Gerald paused for a second.
'**I'm not a fish,**' he said.

'I'm a
whale!'

The blue fish
seemed impressed.

'Hey everyone, come and meet Tiny Whale!'

'I thought whales
would be bigger.'

Gerald stayed with the blue fish all day,
enjoying the attention and telling tall
tales, until it was time to go home.

The next day, Gerald returned, and soon there
was a big crowd of blue fish listening to his stories.

'Hey guys, it's
Tiny whale!'

'Is it true
you once jumped
over a ship?'

'How big is
your mum?'

Gerald stayed for tea, which was pretty
much like tea at home, but bluer.
All the fish gathered in a cosy cave
with a small entrance at the top.
Gerald was introduced to the
oldest and wisest fish of all.
He wore a red headscarf
and an eyepatch, and he
squinted and blinked
as he listened to
Gerald's stories.

Gerald didn't like the suspicious look in his eye.
It seemed like a good time to go home.

But it wasn't long before Gerald decided to visit his new friends again. However, this time, when he arrived at the blue fishes' reef, it was quiet and empty.

Where was everybody?

Gerald thought he heard a noise ... and then he saw it ...
a huge boulder sat right on top of the entrance
to the blue fishes' cave!

An eye appeared in a crack at the bottom
of the boulder - it was one of the blue fish!

'Hey, Tiny Whale,' he said. 'Is that you?
We're all trapped beneath this boulder.
Thank goodness you're here, can you
move it? We're SO lucky we made
friends with a whale!'

'Um, yep,'
said Gerald,
'lucky I'm a whale.
This should be easy.'

Gerald strained and pushed
until his muscles shook.
But the boulder
didn't move.

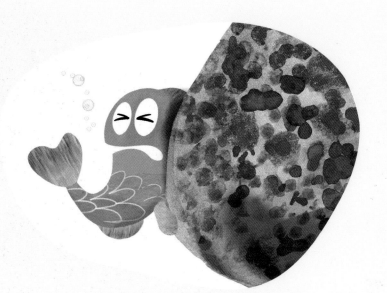

Gerald pushed and strained until
his flippers went floppy.
But still the boulder
didn't move.

'Wait there,' he shouted
down the crack.
'I'll be right back!'

Gerald swam faster than he'd ever swum
before and soon he was back home.

'Stop everybody!' he yelled.
'Listen!'

But nobody stopped.
'Listen!' he shouted.

But no one listened.

Gerald picked
up a shell ...

'LISTEN!'

he trumpeted.

Everybody listened.

'Hey, it's Godfrey!'

'I really need everybody's help,' said Gerald. 'Quick, follow me!'

The entire school of orange fish sped across
the seabed with Gerald leading the way.

Gerald

None of the creatures in the sea had
ever seen anything like it before!

'We need to move this boulder. There are fish trapped beneath it,' said Gerald.

'**Ready?**' he called.

'**NOW!**'

The fish pushed ...

and pushed ...

and pushed.

The boulder moved a tiny bit, then a little bit more, and then, with a sea-shuddering crash, it rolled away from the cave!

Out of the cave streamed hundreds
of cheering blue fish.

'We're free!'

'Yippee!'

'Wooooooooo!'

The oldest and wisest blue fish came swimming slowly towards Gerald.

'Thank you, Tiny Whale,' he said, and gave Gerald his headscarf.

'But how did you recognise me?' asked Gerald.

'Hooray!'

'Hip hip hooray!'

'Because you're the only whale!' said the old fish,
as he blinked, or maybe winked. It was difficult to tell.

Everybody cheered! Gerald couldn't believe it ...

Finally, everybody knew who he was!

'Can you
spot Gerald?'